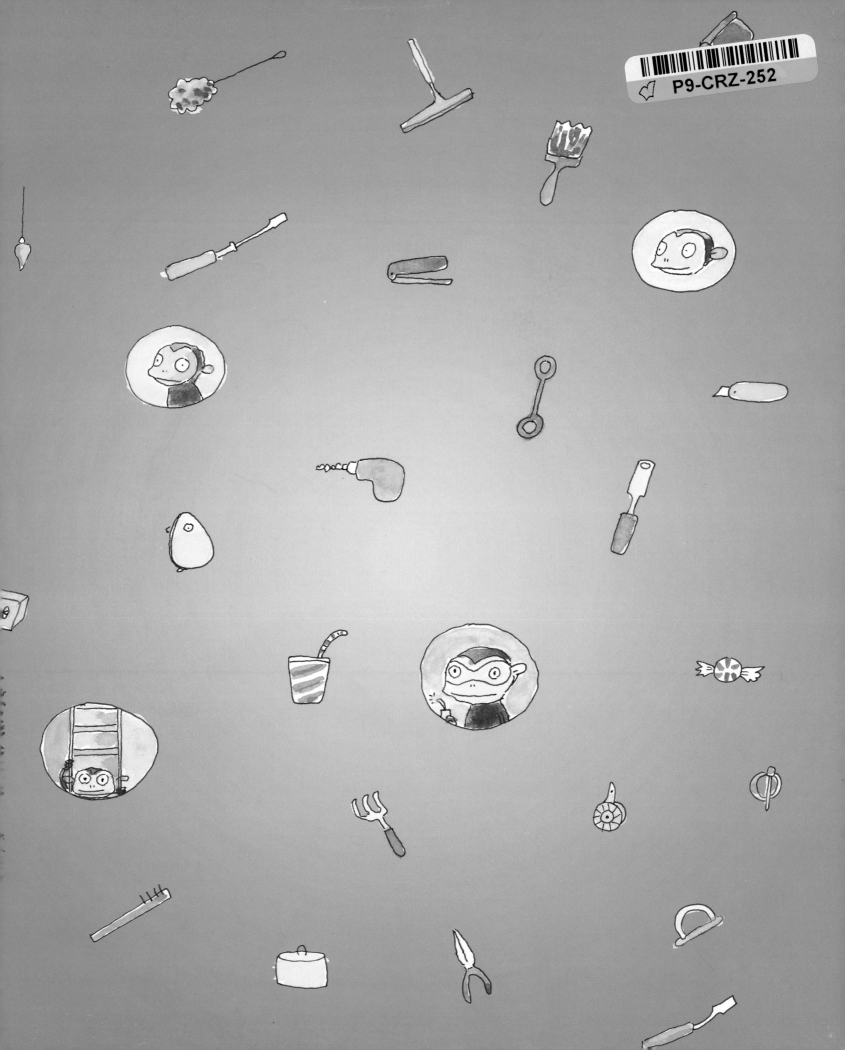

Monkey With A Tool Belt

And The NOISY PROBLEM

Chris Monroe

CAROLRHODA BOOKS MINNEAPOLIS · NEW YORK

To Vern and Gary — CM

Carolrhoda Books
A division of Lerner Publishing Group, Inc.
241 First Avenue North
Minneapolis, MN 55401 U.S.A.

Website address: www.lernerbooks.com

Library of Congress Cataloging-in-Publication Data

Monroe, Chris.
    Monkey with a tool belt and the noisy problem / by Chris Monroe.
        p.   cm.
    Summary: When Chico the monkey wakes up to a loud clatter, he puts on his tool belt and searches his tree house to find what is making the noise, only to discover Clark the elephant stuck in the laundry chute.
    ISBN: 978-0-8225-9247-1 (lib. bdg. : alk. paper)
    [1. Monkeys—Fiction. 2. Elephants—Fiction. 3. Tools—Fiction.] I. Title.
    PZ7.M76OMon 2009
    [E]—dc22   2008025891

Manufactured in the United States of America
1 2 3 4 5 6 — JR — 14 13 12 11 10 09

AROOGA BOOM CLANG CLANG

Early one morning, **Chico Bon Bon**
awoke to a **loud noise** in his tree house.

"What could that be?" he wondered, as he jumped out of bed and straightened his **tool belt**.

AROOGA BOOM CLANG CLANG

some of Chico's tools

chopper
chipper
bopper
bipper
tacker
clacker
snicker-snacker
nail finder
candy finder
plug wrench
lug wrench
pug wrench
bug wrench

razzler
frazzler
frizzler
twizzler
de-twizzler
lid lifter
pickle picker
jibber
jabber
paper scraper
glitter vac
putty splapper
tail clamp
sponge brush
hook-on-a-stick

He had every tool
a monkey would ever need.

AROOGA BOOM CLANG CLANG

There it was again! "It must be the wind," Chico thought.
A strong wind WAS blowing through his bedroom window.

He shut the window and pulled his screwdriver
from his tool belt to reattach the curtain rod
that had blown off the wall.

"The wind can be very loud sometimes,"
he said to himself.

Chico heard the noise **17** times during breakfast.
"I'm not sure that IS the wind after all."

Chico decided to investigate.

He took his hear-a-lot tool from his belt
and put it up to the wall.

He checked in the bread box.

He peeked in the hamper.

AROOGA BOOM
BOOM
CLANG
CLANG

He pried up the floorboards
with a snozzle and clamper.

He climbed up a pole.

He dove in
the pool.

He looked under the stairs
with a stair-staring tool.

But he couldn't find the noise.

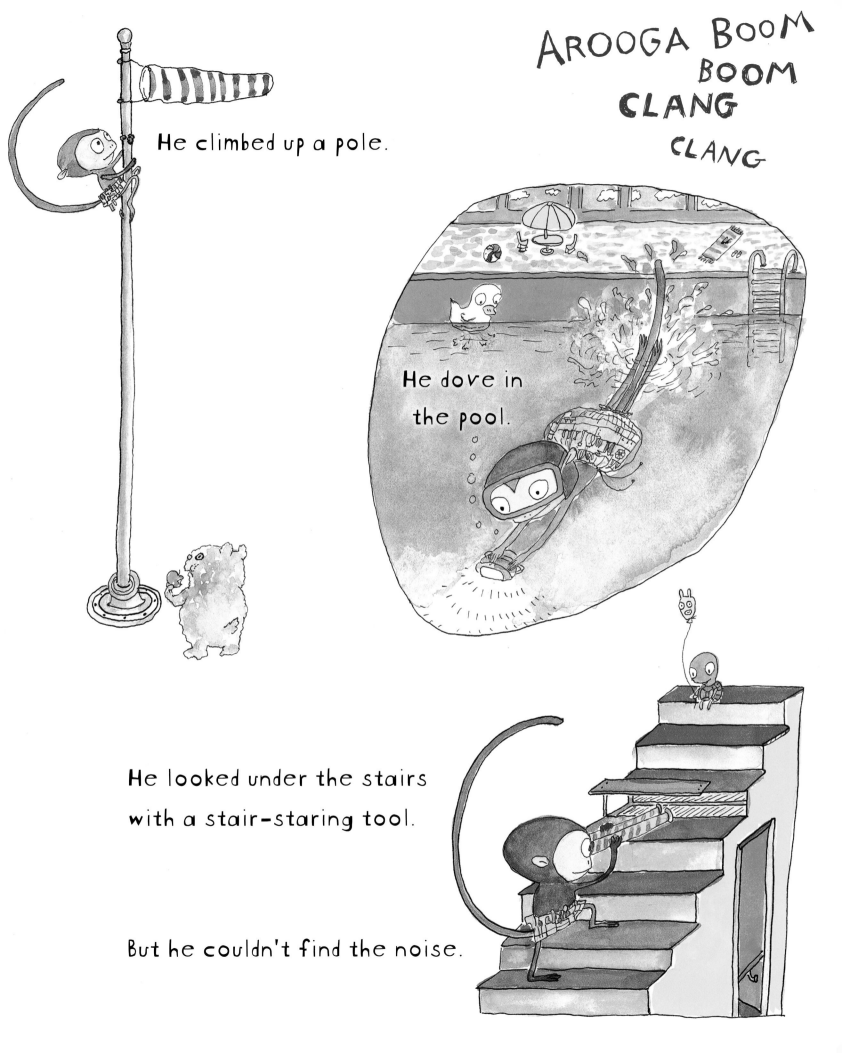

Chico sat on the steps to think.

Was the Woodpecker family
playing a trick on him?

Was someone chopping
his tree into firewood?

Were there bats
in the belfry?

Was it a monster?

Had a family of very loud squirrels moved in?

Had a spacecraft landed on the roof?

Was there a **TERMITE PROBLEM?**

"This could be serious," Chico thought. He put on his safety goggles and continued the hunt.

But Chico couldn't use his tools to FIX the noisy problem, because he couldn't FIND the noisy problem.

Chico stopped in the hallway and took his hankie
from his tool belt. He wiped off his face.
(He had gotten very dirty while searching,
especially when he went up the chimney.)

He opened the laundry chute door.
Just as he was dropping in the hankie,
the noise echoed up the chute.

Chico rubbed his ears. "I think I found the noise," he said. He plugged his earplugs into his ears and put on his hard hat. Then he bravely peered down the chute.

It was very dark.

Chico shone his 100-watt flashlight down the hole. But all he could see was his hankie, a pair of shorts, and a beach towel jammed in the chute.

Something was stuck in there.

"I should go down to the laundry room and look up," thought Chico.

Which is what he did . . .

and this is what he saw. . . . .

An elephant was
clogging his
laundry chute.

"I'll have to build her one," thought Chico.

But for now, he set to work to get Clark out.

① He measured the distance to Clark with his tape measure.

② Using his pencil, he divided by 7.

③ He made 3 cuts in the edge of the chute with his 3-cut saw.

④ He sanded the inside of the chute with his sliver-stopper sander.

⑤ He thought about using his XL grease gun to squirt grease around Clark's edges but changed his mind.

⑥ "Too messy," he thought. "It might get all over my laundry."

7. He decided to go with Plan B.

8. He went to the kitchen and came back with 12 bananas. He began peeling and eating them one by one.

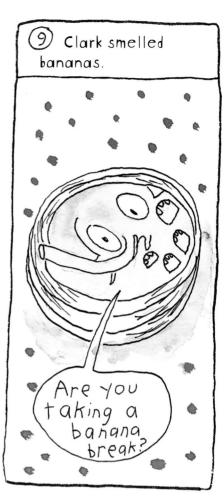

9. Clark smelled bananas.

Are you taking a banana break?

10. Chico put the banana peels into his newly built banana cannon and shot them up the chute.

It's part of my plan.

11. Then he used his edge-wedger to wedge the slippery peels around Clark's edges.

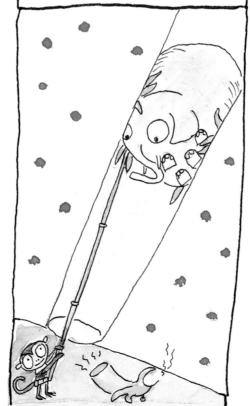

12. Finally, he attached a sticky winch to Clark's foot and pulled with all his might. He pulled and pulled and suddenly . . .

Clark broke free and slid down the chute, landing with a giant **THUD** on the laundry pile.

"Thank you!" said Clark. "That was really uncomfortable. Also, **VERY LOUD**."

"Yes," said Chico. "It really was."

Chico wanted to ask Clark just exactly
HOW he had gotten into the laundry chute.
But he thought that might be rude.

And Clark said, "Yes, please!"

So they sat down to a peanut butter-banana feast.

"Good thing you have that tool belt," said Clark.

"Yes," said Chico. "It's very handy."

And he did.